Remember the King

Also by Jacob English

Christianity 101: Things You Wish Your Pastor Told You

Remember the King

A CHRISTIAN ALLEGORY OF GREATNESS

JACOB ENGLISH

RISE UP
PUBLICATIONS

Book design by eBook Prep
www.ebookprep.com

January 2023
ISBN: 978-1-64457-605-2

Rise UP Publications
644 Shrewsbury Commons Ave
Ste 249
Shrewsbury PA 17361
United States of America
www.riseUPpublications.com
Phone: 866-846-5123

PART ONE

Identity

Chapter One

BORN WITH PURPOSE

"Before I formed thee in the belly I knew thee; and before thou camest forth out of the womb I sanctified thee and ordained thee a prophet unto the nations."

— JEREMIAH 1:5 KJV

For God does not show favoritism.

— ROMANS 2:11 NIV

I have wondered in times past—as I'm sure many have—if there is an actual purpose to life. I have found an overwhelming answer in the scriptures as God reveals His truth about us. We are all known by God before we arrive on planet earth. He knows us as His children, and He has sent us into the earth for us to rediscover and fulfill His will.

Before any person is born, they first had an origin with God. I want this to be understood: Before you were formed and existed in the flesh, God knew you and ordained you. He didn't know you by thought, He didn't know you in His mind, He knew you as a person, and He ordained you to be sent into the earth for this specific time. He had a specific plan in mind when He sent you here. You were destined to become someone significant in His kingdom and to accomplish great things. Who can be ordained before they are known? Who can be known before they are alive? What if I told you that you were alive in spirit before you came here and you even knew God? You came out of eternity; you are an eternal being, which is why you will spend eternity in Heaven or Hell.

The Bible goes as far as saying that God hid His kingdom within us. We all have God's divine will hiding within us that we have been born to accomplish. No one on this planet was born without a Godly purpose. No one was born to be destroyed—as many theologians misinterpret the scripture. Every single person was born to accomplish God's specific will, and God has no evil within Him, nor does He orchestrate evil. There is no favoritism in God towards people. We were all designed with a Godly purpose hidden within.

Chapter Two

LOST KNOWLEDGE

Many of us cannot see our purpose—even though God clearly created us for a purpose—because of sin. The Bible says that Adam walked with God in the cool of the day, but on the day that he sinned, Adam hid from God. Why would Adam hide from a God he knew sincerely as his father? That was the question God asked him. *"Who told you that you were naked? Have you partaken of the tree of the knowledge of good and evil?"* The Bible says Adam was afraid of God and hid from Him. In truth, Adam had a new sinful mind. After all, the fruit was "the fruit of the KNOWLEDGE of good and evil."

Adam, through sin, gained new knowledge. He had a new mind capable of evil things. This took away Adam's old knowledge, which was the knowledge of the purpose God gave him—to subdue the earth, multiply and have dominion. This has been the case with all of mankind because of sin. We can never see God's plan for us if sin remains.

The Bible states that we are all born in sin. If we are born in sin, we are also born in a sinful state of mind. Just as God separated Adam from walking with Him in the garden, so are our minds removed from His presence in a sinful state. We have a purpose within us, but we do not know it. We cannot find or see our purpose if we are in sin.

In sin, we are separated from God, and by this separation, we have also been separated from our eternal purpose because our purpose is found only in Him. Therefore, we feel empty and unsatisfied when trying to accomplish things independently. There is always a "what's next." We have not lost our purpose; the Bible declares that God will not take away His call on our lives, but until we surrender to God, we cannot know our purpose.

Without redemption, we will never know who we really are. One can be created and ordained to do tremendous things for God but miss it because the mind stays hidden from God's plans throughout life.

Jesus will tell those in sin to depart. "I never knew you." It is sad to think that one day we will return to God, and many will say they have done great things in His name, yet He will tell them to depart because of their iniquity. Iniquity is sin. If sin remains, we may accomplish great things, but they will not be the accomplishment of our God-ordained purpose.

This is a tough statement to understand when we see that He says He knows us and ordains us before we enter the world. We recognize through this statement that we have the potential to miss God's plan for our lives and become something He never intended us to be—someone He doesn't know.

When the appointed time comes for us to go be with the Lord, He will be looking for that man or woman whom He knew and ordained before they were sent into the earth to do His will. Will He recognize you as who He created you to be? Are you doing what God has called you to do? That is the only thing that matters in life. The ones who have done His will are the ones who will hear "Well done."

Chapter Three

ENLIGHTENMENT

God did not want us to remain separate from Him or His purpose for our lives, so He sent our powerful Savior, Jesus Christ, as the light of the world. He came to reveal the truth to us. What truth? The truth of His kingdom, the truth of His spirit, and the truth of His will for us. He said that He came that the blind might see and that those who see might be made blind. Jesus wants to enlighten us about our purpose in Him and cause worldly purpose to dim. He is a light unto our purpose. He says He is the door...the door to what? The doorway into God's kingdom, where we are ambassadors for Him, accomplishing His purpose. He is the doorway to our purpose!

While we are all born in sin, Jesus came declaring a way to restore our original purpose in God. He says we must be born again (saved) to see the kingdom (your purpose) and that we must be born of the spirit and of water to enter into His kingdom (your purpose). This may sound confusing, so let me explain further. The Bible declares that God's kingdom is within you. When we lost our ability to know God's will for us, we died to His will, but His will did not die; only our ability to understand it in our flesh died. He hid His will for us within our spirit man, but He wants to reveal to us this great mystery of His kingdom.

When we are born again, we cannot understand our purpose in our flesh, but we begin to feel like we are not empty anymore. We feel like we are doing what we have always been meant to do. Salvation is the beginning of fulfilling your purpose, and we feel His presence tremendously at the point of conversion. We no longer see with our natural eyes; we see by faith—God's first step in His purpose for our lives.

The next steps come through seeking the baptism of His Spirit. Jesus said that when the Holy Spirit came, He would lead us into all "truth" …truth about what? His kingdom, His power in us, and His will for our lives. The Holy Spirit gives power not just to see the doorway of salvation but also to see that God has a kingdom He wants us to enter. He has a purpose for us that can only be discovered through His Spirit.

Many of us have had experiences where we felt the Spirit of God prompting us to do something. When we obey Him, something in us is stirred up. In our natural mind, we may feel crazy or uncomfortable at first, but upon obedience, we feel the presence of God overwhelm us. This is because in our natural mind, because of sin, we can never see God's will. We died to that when Adam fell, but in the Spirit, we can see. We may not understand why we must do what the Spirit leads us to do at a certain place or time, but when we obey Him, a celebration breaks loose within us because our spirit, where God's purpose is hidden, is telling us, "You are finally walking in the purpose you were meant to walk in, all along!" When our spirit becomes one with God's Spirit, we rediscover His will for us.

Walking in obedience to the Holy Spirit, being sensitive to His voice, and pursuing Him with everything in us is the only way to complete our purpose. Our natural mind can only know partly because of the sin battling our minds. But the Lord says in His Word, even when we don't know everything we are supposed to do, He will always tell us what our next steps are— He guides our every step.

Chapter Four

UNDERSTANDING BIBLICAL PURPOSE

E very God-given purpose aligns with the five categories that God instituted in His Word. There are no other offices of purpose. They may not always be glorified in the same light, but they are the only areas of calling. These areas are referred to as the fivefold ministry. Many people say they feel called to raise their kids, or they feel called to write music and sing, or called to this or called to that. They may 'feel' that way, but they are speaking out of their own desires. God's calling happens before you are on this planet. It came here with you. Therefore, it cannot be something you gain here on earth. It's not your kids, it's not your job, and it's not your music or dance. It is a direct office revealed in the fivefold ministry.

Each office carries a significant anointing. There are no *small* offices. If you are a teacher, but you want to be an apostle and you attempt to be an apostle instead of doing your call, first, you will never be one. Secondly, you will make a fool of yourself and become a mockery of God's purpose for your life. Be who you were called to be. Don't try to impersonate preachers you like. Be you in God.

In the fivefold ministry, there are prophets, evangelists, pastors, teachers, and apostles. These are not offices in a church, while many leaders in churches may operate in the office or offices of these callings. These are the divisions of the body of Christ. Think of them as military branches, all fighting for the Lord's army, with different special areas of operation. You are absolutely called into one of them.

Each calling operates in any gift of the Spirit as needed. All of the gifts of the Spirit are listed as this: speaking in tongues, interpretation of tongues, prophecy, discerning of spirits, faith, healing, working of miracles, word of wisdom, and word of knowledge.

One of these offices is mantled within every person alive to establish God's kingdom, which happens only through destroying the kingdom of the Devil. You are called to be a fighter and an overcomer for God's kingdom. In other words, doing God's will makes you the Devil's number one enemy. To set up God's kingdom, you must destroy Satan's kingdom. You will undoubtedly do this, so long as you are apt to listen to the Spirit and do His will as He shows you how to defeat the enemy.

Teachers will teach the Word, unfolding God's revelation to His people. Pastors will gather a flock and must have the vision to do so. If you have no idea where you are taking a church and no clear vision of where the ministry you lead must go, resign immediately; you are not a pastor. Evangelists will go from place to place, preaching the truth, breaking ground that hasn't been broken, and preparing the way for God's kingdom (church) to be planted in a new place. Prophets will often seem strange, but they will warn the body of what will come. They will know things only the Holy Spirit can show them. Apostles are church planters and overseers. They will touch all five gifts of the fivefold ministry frequently in their lives.

There is no small office in the body. There is no small calling over your life. You were created to do more than exist. You were meant to wreak havoc on the kingdoms of Hell and uproot them so that the kingdom of God can take over, everywhere you go.

PART TWO
Remember the King

Prelude

As I studied patiently and prayed for the Lord to help me paint a picture to help you understand how God's call on a person's life operates holistically, I wrote a short allegory that I believe will help you more fully grasp the cycle of life—where we are from, what we are meant to do, and how we are to address our call in the Lord. You may not understand your calling in the Lord fully, but I assure you, you are called to do great things.

Chapter Five

BEFORE

Far above the clouds and beyond the stars, there exists a great kingdom filled with light. What a beautiful kingdom it is, ornate with every type of beautiful jewel. It has twelve gates made of jasper and golden streets, made of more pure gold than has ever been seen. It is a vast kingdom, filled with laughter and joy, incomparable to any other kingdom that has ever been known.

At the center of this kingdom is the most royal palace and, within it, a great white throne. Here the King sits to rule over His kingdom. Out of His throne shines a great and beautiful light. It illuminates the whole city so that there is no darkness at all, not even a shadow. From His throne, a river as clear as crystal pours through the middle of the city. All those who live in the city drink of this river, they never age, and are without pain or ailment.

One day, as the King sat on his throne, He gathered His children and told them stories of another realm where He built a separate kingdom. He told them stories of many of His children whom He has already sent to the other realm and how they returned and now live in beautiful golden mansions, ruling over cities within His kingdom. He pointed to the many mansions built near His palace and told stories of how His children became great and how proud He is of them.

Looking across the sea of subjects, His holy children listening intently, He told them they too can be great. He would send anyone willing to go to His other kingdom and help build it.

But His children were afraid to go because they knew of the great dragon that imposed rule in His other kingdom. Some of His children had gone and never returned, having become a servant of the dragon. Still, the King had great confidence in all His children, and He asked if anyone was willing to go and help prepare His other kingdom, for the day He merges the two kingdoms and rules them both.

As He beckoned His children, a young man stood. He was young and strong, with dark hair. He said to the King, "Father, I will go. Send me."

The King motioned him to come close to His throne and explained to him what the other kingdom was like and what he must do there.

"My son, I must warn you, this kingdom is of another realm. When you enter this kingdom, you will not remember being from here. You will deal with things that pertain to that realm because you have an enemy there, a great dragon. Your enemy tricked the first ones I sent into this realm. Because of that, there is a curse placed on the mind of every person sent so they don't remember Me or where they are from.

"I'm not sending you alone, so don't worry. I have hidden parts of your memory and the power that belongs to you as My son, within My Spirit. My Spirit, called the Holy One, will be with you everywhere you go. He is already waiting for you. Once you arrive, I will arrange a meeting with Him.

"When you meet with Him, as He speaks, you will remember Me in your heart. If you listen to Me, I will show you where to go and how to prepare My kingdom for Me.

"I've hidden the tools to build My kingdom within you. You won't be left unequipped. However, the dragon knows this, so he will try to distract you with many things that have nothing to do with the kingdom to steal your power from you and enslave you.

"To keep you centered, I've already sent your elder brother to establish my words as law in this kingdom. When you speak the words I have established there, the curse will be lifted off of your mind and My Spirit will show up to fight for you.

"I've also instructed guardians to protect and help you in times of need. Whenever you speak My Word, you can tell the guardians what you need help with, and they will always help you.

"Many things of this kingdom will remain unseen in the other realm until you speak My Word. As you speak My Word, things that are from this kingdom will be created there. You will learn to operate in My ways and you will do great things."

With the King's description of what was to come, He asked his son, "Are you ready to go?"

The son responded with an eager smile and a confident nod.

Placing His hand on a crimson curtain, The King pulled it back, revealing a portal through which the young man saw a woman and a man.

"Who are these, Father?"

The King answered, "These are the two people that I've already sent. They are establishing My kingdom even now. You will be in their care and instruction until you can rule on your own. Don't be afraid. You are going to do great things. I have already set things in place for you."

With this, the young man went through the portal to awaken, as a baby, in the new realm.

Chapter Six

SENT

Raised in a rural area filled with cattle, sheep, and beautiful clear night skies, the twelve-year-old boy, named Phillip, tended to his father's sheep and cattle as dusk began to settle in. Upon the arrival of the stars in the dimming sky, Phillip quickly finished his chores and ate dinner with his parents and his older brothers.

After dinner every night, his mother pulled out a book called "The Holy Word," which told of another kingdom with a great King who watches over His children. Phillip's father told him and his brothers that the book is true and that one day the King will come. He told them that anyone who obeys the King's words, as written in "The Holy Word," is His child. "Until the King comes, we are here making ready for Him." As his father described the soon-coming King, a sense of familiarity burned within Phillip, who always loved hearing about the King.

During the day, Phillip wrote songs about the King and sang them as he tended the livestock.

One night, Phillip's mother began to read a story about another young man in the Holy Word. The story began with the King saying, "Before I formed you in the womb, I knew you; before you were born, I sanctified you; I ordained you a prophet to the nations."

Phillip pondered the thought of being known before he was formed. He asked his father, "How can you be known before you are born?"

To which his father replied, "The King knows us all before we were ever here. He is the One who sent us here."

Although it was hard for Phillip to fathom being known before he was in this realm, he considered what it would be like to know the King of the Holy Word as he fell asleep. Sleepily, he repeated the text that was read to him, "Before I formed you in the womb, I knew you; before you were born, I sanctified you; I ordained you a prophet to the nations" as he drifted off to sleep.

Suddenly, Phillip found himself in an all-white room with a man who appeared to glow brightly. He couldn't see the man's face, only that he was dressed in white, and his skin glowed like shining brass. Immediately, Phillip felt better than he had ever felt before, and he was filled with joy. He squinted his eyes at the bright visage of the man, and he asked, "Lord, who are you?"

The man replied in a thunderous yet gentle voice, "I am the King."

"The king?" Phillip asked. "What king?"

"The King of the Holy Word." replied the Lord. "I've come to show you who you really are—who you have always been. Tomorrow morning you will meet a man I have sent to anoint you. You will be given great strength and courage to stop the dragon's reign in your land."

At the end of this message, the room went completely dark. Phillip closed his eyes and opened them again. He found himself back in his room, lying in his bed. *"Was this just a dream?"* he asked himself. *"It couldn't be; it was so real."* Sleepy and perplexed, Phillip lay down and drifted back to sleep.

Early the next morning, Phillip was out in the field watching the cattle when a man arrived at his house. This man was a prophet, well known in the land as the spokesman of the Great King. He was the one the King spoke to, by His Spirit, to anoint the barons over the provinces of the land. Everything the prophet spoke always came to pass.

The prophet walked into the house and told Phillip's mother and father that the Great King had sent him to anoint a new baron over their lands and that it was one of their sons. The parents excitedly lined up all their sons side-by-side, except for Phillip, who was taking care of the livestock.

The prophet appeared perplexed, leading the father to ask, "Is something wrong, sir?"

The prophet answered, "None of these is the one the King has sent me to anoint. Do you have any other sons?"

The father said, "We have only one other son. He's just a boy, out tending to the sheep and the cattle. We will send for him."

Upon the arrival of Phillip, the prophet immediately smiled. Without warning, the prophet took a vial of oil and poured it onto Phillip's head, declaring over him, "As spoken by the King Himself to me, you are anointed to be strong and to crush the head of the dragon in these lands. You will be baron, for you have a heart like the King's heart. From this day forward, whenever you call on the King, He will send His Spirit to fight for you and He will station guardians around you, and nothing shall by any means harm you." Then the prophet left abruptly.

Phillip's older brothers, though seemingly jealous, congratulated him on the word spoken over him. From this day forward, Phillip began to hear the voice of the King instruct him from within, and he became very brave and very strong.

Chapter Seven
UNDERSTANDING THE CALL

P hillip got stronger and stronger each day. On the day of Phillip's seventeenth birthday, Richard, the current baron of the land, declared war with the other barons in surrounding lands who were under the influence of the great dragon. Phillip's brothers were out warring against the enemies of the Great King because Phillip was not yet old enough to go to war. He was anxious to fight for the King, but as of now, he was still taking care of the sheep and the cattle.

Because of the impending war, many grotesque creatures came out of the camps of the dark surrounding lands looking to pillage and rob the homes left unattended or occupied by those too weak to fight. One day, two large and hideous beasts wandered onto Phillip's field while he was tending his sheep and cattle. The beasts seized two sheep and attempted to steal and eat them.

Phillip was angered and called upon the King for strength. "Great King, let Your hand be upon my enemies and give me great strength!" Immediately, he was filled with strength and boldness. He grabbed those wicked beasts by their hair and smote them until they were dead.

Shortly after this attack, Phillip's father sent him with food for his brothers and to see how they were faring. If the attacks were happening here, there was no telling what his brothers were facing in the heat of the battle; his father feared the worst.

After a few days' journey, he arrived on the mountainside and saw soldiers hiding in the trees and behind rocks, terribly afraid. Even the baron was hiding in a cave. Phillip began asking some of the soldiers why they were hiding. About the time he started to get answers, a twelve-foot tall, dark dragon covered in scales walked into the valley of battle. This was not the great dragon, but the great dragon sent him to conquer the land where Phillip lived. He breathed fire and spoke curses against the Great King.

The dragon spoke, "There is no need for you all to die. Send me your greatest warrior. If he can defeat me, we will be your slaves...but if I defeat him, this land will belong to us, and you will serve the great dragon and us."

When Phillip heard this from the dragon, he was furious. Immediately, he heard the voice of the King within him saying, *"Be bold; you will defeat him. I am with you."* Immediately, Phillip left the hiding place and challenged the dragon, "I will fight you!"

The dragon scoffed. "You are merely a child. I will kill you in the name of the great dragon and feed you to my beasts."

Phillip shouted, "Today I will defeat you because you have spoken against the Great King. All will see the power of the Great King today! By His Spirit, I will take your head, and all will know there is a King in this land."

Immediately Phillip ran at the dragon with a sword in his hand. The dragon let out a terrifying roar, breathing fire out of his mouth. Phillip ran through the fire but wasn't burned. He came to the dragon, leaped at him, and with all his might, thrust the sword right through the dragon's heart.

The dragon cried out and staggered, falling to the ground, breathing his last. Phillip took the sword and, with one swoop, cut off the dragon's head.

The Great King's army roared with a voice of triumph and charged the army of the dragon, and they fled from before them. Phillip lifted the head of the dragon and threw it at the feet of the baron, Richard.

Richard asked Phillip, "Where do you live?"

"I live at home with my parents, and I tend their sheep and cattle."

Richard replied, "From now on, you will not live at home with your parents. You will live with me in the baron's palace."

At this instruction, Phillip moved immediately into the baron's palace and was appointed a captain in the royal army.

Chapter Eight

GROWING IN THE CALL

P hillip grew in the baron's palace, becoming greater and greater. He won many battles in and out of the cities and lands, so much so that the people grew to love him and see him as their champion.

At first, Richard had no problem with this and even admired Phillip as a son, but as Phillip gained success, strength, and admiration, Richard became very jealous of him.

"Why do the people love him so much?" Richard thought. It wasn't that long ago that Richard was anointed by the Great King's prophet to be baron himself. The problem was, whenever Richard heard the voice of the King speaking to him in times past, he often ignored the voice of the King and did what he thought was best.

Once, when the prophet was going to speak at an annual festival celebrating the Great King, he was held late in communication with the Great King as to what he should say to the people. Rather than waiting for the prophet, Richard stood in for him without the King's permission. This displeased the King. It was unholy for Richard to assume a position he wasn't anointed for. After disobeying the King's voice on several other occasions, the Great King regretted choosing Richard and anointed Phillip to be the next baron of the land in Richard's place.

Richard was now reaping the effects of his disobedience. He wasn't hearing the voice of the Great King anymore. His boldness turned to bitterness and he became jealous of Phillip because the Great King had chosen Phillip to take his place.

Upon one of Phillip's ventures into battle, as he came back into the city, the people cheered and sang of Phillip's great conquests. When Richard heard the people singing about Phillip and his greatness, he was filled with rage and conspired against him in hopes that the people would reject him. Richard proclaimed that Phillip was an enemy of the Great King. He sent soldiers after Phillip to capture him so he could kill him and remain baron. Phillip narrowly escaped and hid in the forests of the land.

As Phillip lived in the forest, all the men who served under him in the royal army left the baron's command to live under the guidance of Phillip. Anyone who was rejected or cast out for speaking in defense of Phillip also came to the forest to live with him. His family joined him, and Phillip became great even in a desolate place. But as Phillip grew in greatness, he refused to fight against Richard because Richard had been anointed by the Great King. Phillip always lived in honor of the Great King's anointed people. He believed that putting a hand on anyone the Great King had anointed was unrighteous.

Although Phillip lived in the forest, he never stopped fighting against the enemies of the Great King. Whenever there was a breach against the land, Phillip was there to destroy the enemy. He wouldn't allow the enemies of the Great King to intrude on the land.

Chapter Nine

FULFILLMENT

For twelve years, Phillip and his army lived in the forest of the land. Richard became weak-minded and afraid. The land's enemies knew of his weakness and under the instruction of the great dragon, the evil armies of the dark lands gathered to attack and invade the Great King's lands.

Phillip fiercely destroyed all the invaders near his encampment, but most of the evil army met Richard on the battlefield, where he was overrun. As Richard and his sons retreated to a high mountain following a fierce and dreadful loss, they were ambushed by the baron's guard. Without warning, the dark archers released their arrows, slaying all of Richard's sons and badly wounding Richard, who managed to retreat behind a large rock, turning his back to lean against it. Peering into the valley of the battle, Richard felt the weight of his disobedience as he watched his kinsmen being destroyed by the dragon's army. But rather than cry out in repentance to the Great King, he drew his sword, bowed his head, and pierced himself through.

When the King's great army heard that Richard was dead, along with all his sons, they fled before the evil armies of the dragon. With no one to lead them, they scattered, fearful of what was coming from the great dragon. They couldn't allow the dragon to overtake the lands of the King. The colony elders of the King's lands gathered to discuss what they should do after the dragon's army burned and pillaged nearly a third of the cities belonging to the King. They needed a leader and knew of no one better able to lead the people than Phillip, the great warrior of the forest.

Immediately, the elders sent a messenger to seek out Phillip and plead that he come and defend the lands of the Great King. The messenger arrived in the forest and was confronted by a watchman who quickly brought the messenger to Phillip. When Phillip heard that Richard and his sons had been killed by the great dragon's armies, he became enraged. Mounting his horse, he rode out to meet with the elders and the captains of the armies of the Great King.

Phillip addressed the counsel of the elders and the royal army, saying: "Richard and his sons were as strong as lions. They were swifter than eagles. They fought valiantly for the Great King. The great dragon has come against the Lord our King and we have all lost our leader, Richard, the King's anointed one. But now, don't be afraid, you mighty men of battle. Be strong and filled with might. Let fear go through the land. May the Great King's enemies tremble, for the King will avenge His anointed! Prepare yourselves, you men of war, kindle your anger against the great dragon and his wicked servants. For today we will be the arm of vengeance for the Lord our Great King and we will drive out and destroy all of the dragon's armies."

As the sound of the royal army's shout bellowed into the enemy's camps, all the dragon's armies heard it. They stopped eating and making merry and all peace left their tents. They were filled with fear because the Holy One, the Spirit of the King, had come upon them, melting their courage.

At midnight, Phillip and the royal infantry charged into the camp of the evil army. With swiftness, the army of the King destroyed the army of the great dragon. Fear of the Great King's vengeance by his servant, Phillip, spread throughout all the dark lands so that the dragon himself was too afraid to ever enter the land.

Chapter Ten

PASSING THE MANTLE

After the victory by the armies of the Great King under Phillip's leadership, all the people and the elders gathered to declare Phillip as the new baron. He was established as the leader of all the Great King's lands. Every colony, city, and town obeyed him as the Great King's chosen baron and the King's anointed.

Phillip continued to command the royal army and further the borders of the Great King's lands. He took much of the great dragon's silver and gold and caused the King's lands to prosper greater than they had ever prospered.

As time passed, Phillip raised up a son, instructed in knowledge by all the elders and wise beyond his years. The Great King loved Phillip's son and blessed him. Through this young man, the Great King built His temple, the place where He would one day appear and merge His two kingdoms.

Phillip fulfilled all that the King spoke to Him in careful obedience until the time came for Phillip to transition rulership to his son. As Phillip conducted his son's coronation, he thanked the Great King for all the wonderful blessings He received, and for the victories wrought through him. He asked the King to do the same and more for his son in his stead.

At the instruction of Phillip, the great assembly stood and thanked the Great King together, saying: "Glory to the King, holy is His name. He is great and worthy to be praised. He has delivered us from all our afflictions; He has healed us from all our diseases. The King's benefits will never be forgotten. All hail the Great King. He is Lord of all. May He come quickly."

Chapter Eleven

GOING BACK HOME

When the ceremony finished, Phillip retired alone to his bed chamber. As he lay on his bed, a man appeared wearing white, his skin glowing like shining brass. Phillip was comforted at the sight of him. The man spoke to Phillip, "It is time for you to go the way of your fathers."

At this, a crimson curtain appeared on the wall. The man pulled back the curtain, revealing a portal through which Phillip saw the most beautiful city he had ever beheld; it looked so familiar to him. Stumbling to his feet, Phillip grabbed the bedpost to stand with one hand, while slowly outstretching his other hand. Feeble in his old age, he stumbled toward the portal. Looking at the man in white, they exchanged a familiar smile. Taking Phillip by the hand, the man in white gently led him through the portal into the great city, and in a flash of light, he was gone.

Phillip's son walked into his father's bed chamber, knowing his father hadn't felt well during the ceremony. As he entered, he caught a glimpse of light as his father crossed through the portal. He called quickly for the royal guard. Upon telling the story to the royal guard and many of Phillip's family as to what he had seen, he wept at the loss of his father. Many of the guards and family members wept sorrowfully, but Phillip's wife did not weep. She consoled her son, telling him that everything was going to be okay. She said, "The Great King has come to take him home. There is no crying where he is; there is only joy in that city." Although many mourn the loss of their beloved leader, Phillip, they cannot help but be encouraged. For they know he is with the King.

Chapter Twelve

REMEMBERING THE KING

As Phillip entered the city, he looked around, slowly beginning to remember.

"Wait a moment, I've been here before. I know this place. Over there are my brothers and sisters—we used to sit in the King's hall together! And over there are my parents-—I haven't seen them since I was a boy! And there are my grandparents! I know this place...I know this place!"

Turning to the man in white clothing, Phillip said, "You...You are the Great King!" Phillip fell to his knees, weeping, overwhelmed with joy and peace.

Smiling, The Great King embraced Phillip. "Yes, Phillip, I am the King and I am so very proud of you. You have done well, My son. Enter into My joy and rest."

Escorted by The Great King, Phillip entered the throne room, surrounded by those he knew in the other realm, and before entering the other realm. They all cheered for him and welcomed him home. The King greatly rewarded Phillip, giving him a crown and many other rewards. He led him to his new mansion very close to the King's palace, where they had a great dinner party honoring Phillip's return. The Great King told Phillip he would forever have a seat at His table and would never again be separated from his loved ones.

Now, as the Great King sits on His throne and asks, "Who will go and establish My kingdom?" He tells of the great victories that His son Phillip and so many others have wrought by His instruction, in the other realm. As He readies His children to cross the threshold into the other realm, He tells them, "In this world, you will have trouble, but don't be afraid, I have overcome the world. I am with you always."

Closing

One day we will all cross back over to that faraway land on the golden strand. Our King is waiting there for us. Our loved ones who did the Lord's will are waiting there for us. Our minds will be able to understand the Lord again. We will remember why we were sent, and we will remember what we were called to do.

Now, we peer through a glass darkly, not seeing the fullness of His call, but one day when we see Him, we will remember what He called us to do. I want to know that I have fulfilled His call for my life. I want to reach as far as I can reach in His Spirit and build His kingdom as high as I possibly can until my appointment to walk through that crimson curtain comes.

In these very last days, God did not send Moses, Elijah, David, Paul, Peter, John, and all the great men of the Bible here; they have previously fulfilled their purpose. In these last days, God didn't wait to send His worst. He has sent His very best to prepare His kingdom for His return—He has sent you. Soon and very soon, we are going to see the King. He's coming soon. Will you be ready?

Today, maybe you think there is no hope; you are too old, or you are too far gone to ever complete your purpose. I've felt the same way that you feel right now, friend, but God redeemed my lost years. The Lord says He will return unto you the years that the cankerworm and the locust and the palmerworm ate away from you. He is a restorer.

You are just as called as you've ever been, but you are faced with a choice. We are not promised forever. The Bible says that life is but a vapor. It is here today and then gone tomorrow. What are you going to do with the time you have left? Will you walk in the call He created you to walk in? Will you yield to the voice of a Father who has never ceased loving you and desires that you come home? Be who He's called you to be. Don't run from Him for another day.

"Father, I ask now that You touch every person reading this book. I pray that even as they read this, Your Spirit falls upon them. Let them know they are loved and that You have never taken Your call from their life. I ask You to restore them to You. I ask You to guide them into Your call for their life. Help them to know that You can take broken things and make them new again, You can use anyone willing to be used by You. I ask You to heal, save and deliver anyone reading this who feels they are unworthy to be who You've called them to be. I thank You that they can be made worthy through the blood of your precious Son, Jesus Christ. Touch them, Father, and bring

them to You. Don't let them rest until they've confessed You as their Lord. In Jesus' name, I pray, Amen."

I sincerely hope this book gives you an enlightened perspective on your eternity with God and how you should approach your walk with Him from now into eternity. May the Lord bless you and keep you, may He shine His face down on you, lift up His countenance over, establish you and give you peace, in Jesus' name.

Christianity 101

For I know the plans I have for you," declares the Lord, "plans to prosper you and not to harm you, plans to give you hope and a future.

— JEREMIAH 29:11 NIV

Understanding God's will for your life comes with also understanding that his purpose for you didn't start after birth. As he told Jeremiah, He also has known you and fore-ordained you for your purpose, specifically in the time that you live in. You are not accidentally here or living in the wrong place or time. God ordained your life for a purpose from heaven and he knew who he wanted you to be before you were born. He designed you with the gifts, talents, and desires for his purpose in you to be completed on the earth.

Neither shall they say, Lo here! or, lo there! for, behold, the kingdom of God is within you.

— LUKE 17:21 KJV

Understand that it is God's will to establish his kingdom on the earth. He uses men and women to do that by creating us with a portion of his kingdom within us. Therefore, it is important not only to become saved but to begin to pursue God's plan for your life and sell out to it. Without pursuing God's Spirit, his kingdom can't be poured out and won't be established.

Available in eBook and paperback from your favorite online retailer or bookstore.

About the Author

Jacob English was raised in an independent Pentecostal ministry and is a fifth-generation preacher. Raised in the quaint southern town of Barnesville, Georgia, he has traveled and ministered since being a teenager and has been in ministry in some form his whole life. Jacob began doing tent revivals during the lockdowns for Covid-19 in 2020. As most churches were closing, he didn't want to stop assembling with believers. Through the leading of the spirit, He felt to start pastoring a church. He currently pastors a church in Reynolds, Georgia with his wife and son, called Living Faith Church, which he started in July 2021. When not writing, he is tending to daily ministry duties, doing ministry podcasts, recording gospel music, or spending quality time with his family. His pastimes still involve gaming and going to the gym.

www.thelivingfaithchurch.com

 facebook.com/jacob.m.english